Lock & Load
A Ryan Lock Short

SEAN BLACK

Edited by Rebecca Cantrell

ISBN: 1481087894
ISBN-13: 978-1481087896

ACKNOWLEDGMENTS

My thanks to Rebecca Cantrell for her editorial assistance. Any errors are entirely mine. I'd also like to thank Joie Simmons for his cover design. Finally, thanks to my family, friends, and readers for their continued support.

ABOUT THIS BOOK

Fresh from an undercover mission inside Pelican Bay Supermax prison in Northern California, close protection operative Ryan Lock and his business partner, Ty Johnson, are in Los Angeles, tasked with protecting a young Hollywood actress from an abusive movie star boyfriend who refuses to accept that their relationship is over. But as Lock knows only too well, and Ty is about to learn, keeping someone safe from harm can be harder than it looks, and damage can come in unexpected forms.

This short story can be read separately from the rest of the Ryan Lock series, as can each full-length novel. For readers following the books in order, the events described here take place between the second book in the series, *Deadlock*, and the third, *Gridlock*.

ONE

WITH HIS HANDS tightening around her neck, choking off her air supply and leaving black shapes clouding her vision, Summer Clements was too damn scared to think about the irony of being strangled to death by her boyfriend. After all, this was precisely how their relationship had started. The difference was that the first time they had been acting.

She had met Jason Durham on the set of a movie called Killing Dawn. Their first scene had called for their characters to have a blazing row. At the end of it, he strangled her to death. Although the scene would appear at the end of the movie, for scheduling reasons it had been their first time together on the set. The indie movie's low-budget hadn't allowed for any rehearsal time and Jason had only become available when a studio film he was due to shoot had fallen through at the last second due to his drinking and substance abuse problems. Now, six months later, with no crew standing around, or cameras rolling to capture the moment for posterity and no director to call cut, it was happening for real.

The fingernails of Jason's right hand dug deep into her neck. He squeezed harder, pinning her against the wall. She felt a breeze tumbling in through the sliding glass doors of the beach house's lower deck but she was no longer sure whether the roar she heard in her ears came from the Pacific

Ocean or the surge of her own blood.

Jason stared at her, his pupils pin prick black against the widescreen backdrop of the Queen's necklace, the curve of coast that ran from Point Dume in the north, through Malibu and all way down to Rancho Palos Verdes in the south. Through the glass she saw the blinking red dots of airplanes taking off from LAX. She wished that she had been smart enough to listen to her friends' advice and jump on one of them. Instead, she had taken his word that he'd never lay a finger on her again, a promise that he'd broken twice.

This time had started like the others, with a dumb argument about nothing. They had been out at a nightclub on the Sunset Strip – Jason trying his best to convince the town that he could still roll with young Hollywood, even though he was pushing fifty up a hill. Her saying hello to a young producer she had worked with a few years back had led to Jason punching the guy. They had been asked to leave.

On the ride back to Malibu, he had fallen into a sullen silence. As she took the ramp onto the 10 freeway, his temper flared.

"You wanted to screw him, right?"

"Will you get a grip? I said 'hello' to the guy."

He lapsed back into silence, which should have been warning enough. Back at the house, she had gone to get a drink from the wet bar.

"Do you want one?" she asked him.

"I'm still waiting for you to answer my question, Summer. Did you want to screw him?"

She knew what was coming next. Her hand shook as she pulled a long-stemmed wine glass from one of the frosted glass bar cabinets and poured herself some Pinot Noir. That was one of the other habits she had picked up since hooking up with Jason – a bottle of wine a night habit to chase down the Ambien she took to get herself to sleep.

"I'm not answering it because it's stupid. Okay, Jason? It's stupid. Too stupid to give you an answer." She took a slug of wine, thinking this was it. She had finally had enough. No amount of bended-knee apologies or flowers or heartfelt love letters would change it. "How many times, Jason?" she went on. "I'm with you, but I'm not going to be if you keep behaving like a jealous asshole."

She could see him in the reflection of the bar cabinets as his eyebrows furrowed. "If I behave like this? We're not talking about me here. We're talking about you."

He was off on a tear now, his voice bouncing off the walls with that Australian accent she had thought was so cute when they had met and that now had the same effect on her as someone drawing their nails down a chalk board.

"Do you know how many women I have throwing themselves at me every single time we go out?"

She rolled her eyes. "I said 'hello' to the guy."

"Sure you said 'hello', but that wasn't what you meant."

Maybe he would sleep it off. She picked up her wine glass. "I'm going to bed."

She walked around the bar and towards the set of stairs on the far side of the house, which led to the master bedroom. As she passed him, he grabbed her wrist. She tried to shake him off, but his grip was too strong.

"I mean it, Jason. I'm done talking about this."

"Well, maybe I'm not," he said.

His lips thinned, his eyes opened, and she knew he had lost it. He let go of her wrist and grabbed her neck. She clawed and scratched at him as he grabbed her with one hand around the throat, and pushed her towards the wall. The more she tried to fight him off, the harder his grip became, until she couldn't breathe. The black spots in her vision grew bigger and merged into a giant mass.

When she came round, she was lying on the floor. He was

sitting on the couch on the opposite side of the room. His head was bowed. He was sobbing, fingers kneading his scalp.

"I'm so sorry. I get jealous. I can't help it. You're so beautiful. I see guys looking at you and I can't handle it."

He got up and started towards her. He reached down and helped her to her feet. She was still too weak to do anything so she let him, but inside she knew that she had to get away from him, for good this time.

TWO

NEXT TO THE word bodyguard, Ryan Lock's least favorite description for his profession had to be bullet catcher. Although sacrificing your life to save the person you were protecting was the ultimate price you might have to pay, close protection work was more a matter of intellect than muscle. In a world that mostly attracted what his former colleagues in the British Royal Military Police's elite close protection unit dubbed 'thick-necked twats', Lock saw himself as more of a problem solver than hired muscle. Right now he was headed to Los Angeles to deal with a rather obstinate Antipodean problem who went by the name of Jason Durham.

"Man, I could get used to this," said Ty Johnson.

Lock glanced over at his six foot four black business partner as Ty stretched out his long legs and waved over a member of the private jet's crew to freshen up his drink. Next to Lock, his fiancee, Carrie, was busy tapping away at her Mac Air, their yellow Labrador, Angel, asleep at her feet. She looked over at him and he smiled.

"You okay, cowboy?"

He leaned in for a kiss. "Better than okay."

Across from them, Ty rolled his eyes. "You two are disgusting."

"Not jealous are you, Tyrone?" Carrie teased.

"Hey, don't even go there, sister."

"I dunno, prison together? I've heard the stories about how that goes. And it's not like I'm saying there's anything wrong with it," she teased.

Ty tutted his disapproval, put his headphones back on and went back to reading his magazine. For his part, Lock was glad that Carrie could find some humor in what had been a terrifying experience for both men when they had recently gone undercover in Pelican Bay Supermax in Northern California.

"You're bad," Lock said, feigning seriousness.

"I know," she said brightly, returning to her work, a story she was fleshing out for her job as a TV reporter back in New York.

Lock dug out a folder of papers outlining his and Ty's latest job and began to review them for the third time. It all looked pretty straightforward – an easy, well paid gig that would tide the business over and pay for his and Carrie's wedding.

The principal – the term used in close protection circles for the person you were actually protecting – was a young actress called Summer Clements. The threat was a highly unpredictable movie star boyfriend called Jason Durham. Durham had grown up in Australia and built his career on a carefully cultivated tough guy image. From what Lock had gathered, the bar for tough guy status in Hollywood wasn't that high. He also suspected the relationship was partly one of convenience. While Summer's career was in the ascendancy, Jason's was a little rocky. He'd had two recent stints in rehab, several arrests, and obviously had, what in modern parlance had come to be known as anger management issues. Lock thought of them more as asshole management issues.

Summer's representatives had contacted Lock directly,

making him a substantial offer for what amounted to a week's work. Not only did they want their young client protected, he also suspected they wanted him to offer a longer term solution by explaining to her ex, by whatever means he felt most appropriate, that the relationship had indeed ended. Saying yes had been a no-brainer.

Lock and Ty could be highly persuasive in such situations, and they both could use the injection of cash. Plus, free first class travel and a pretty heavy stipend that included hotel accommodation and a separate place for Lock and Carrie (a beach house in Malibu owned by the actress) hadn't sounded too shabby either. More than that, if there was one thing that Lock didn't have any time for it was guys like Jason Durham. Over the years he had seen the havoc wreaked by men who abused their partners, and while he wasn't sure what the long term solution was, he was happy to make the world a little better one asshole at a time.

As Ty went to collect their rental car, Lock waited with Carrie. She had a get-together planned with a former colleague who had relocated from New York to Los Angeles a few years ago to work for a rival TV network. That would leave Lock free to go meet Summer and get a better feel for what he was dealing with.

He slipped a hand around his fiancee's waist. Their relationship hadn't been without its bumpy patches, most of which were related to his work, but he still felt like the luckiest man alive. Carrie was beautiful inside and out, a strong woman who knew her own mind, yet hadn't allowed her career to render her cynical about the rest of the human race. He couldn't wait to begin their life together. They already had the dog, who was busy trying to eat the end of the lead and now they could go for the rest of the package; the house with a white picket fence and, hopefully, kids. They'd both had a life spent on the move. Now they craved some quiet domesticity.

Ty pulled up in the rental car, a black Range Rover while Lock helped a taxi driver with Carrie's luggage and kissed her goodbye. He waited until the cab was out of sight, put Angel in the back, and clambered in next to Ty who took off at speed as they headed for West Hollywood.

THREE

IT WAS ONE in the afternoon and the pool of the Chateau Marmont was crowded with hip, young Hollywood player types and girls sporting bikinis that seemed to barely qualify as clothing. Down the years the Chateau had been the bolt hole of choice for Hollywood's elite when they wanted to escape without actually leaving town. It oozed class, discretion, and money. As the old saying went, if you had to ask what it cost to stay there, you probably couldn't afford it.

Lock had Angel on the lead next to him and was wishing he'd brought a spare, complete with shock collar, for Ty.

"Eyes front, Tyrone," said Lock as they skirted round a pair of sun loungers that appeared to come complete with their own Victoria's Secret model. "We're now officially on duty."

Ty's neck swiveled round, and Lock saw himself reflected in the mirrored lenses.

"How you know what I'm looking at? I'm wearing shades, dawg."

"That's how I know. If a man doesn't want anyone to know what he's staring at, he wears shades. Now, can you focus? This is business."

Ty gave a dismissive tut, clearly yet to be convinced that there was any gravity to this particular job. "This movie dude's like five four in his high heels. We're window dressing."

Lock was starting to get irritated at his partner's casual attitude. There was a free table with a couple of chairs. Lock pulled one out and motioned for Ty to take a seat beside him as they waited for their meeting.

He opened the client/principal folder and produced a photograph. "Window dressing, huh?"

He placed the photograph on the glass surface of the table and slid it over to Ty. It showed Summer's neck after the last assault by her former boyfriend. Red welts from where his fingernails had dug into her flesh blushed scarlet against her pale skin. Given how close she had been to a complete blackout, she was lucky to be alive.

Ty looked at it. He grimaced. "Like to see him try that shit with me," he said, taking off his sunglasses and putting them in his shirt pocket, the point clearly taken. He glanced back at the photograph. "She file a complaint?"

Lock shook his head. It wasn't unusual for victims of domestic violence not to file a complaint or press charges. The usual dynamic was that if they, or a neighbor or relative, called it in, then by the time the cops got there the worst part was over and the perpetrator was busy promising their victim the earth if they just gave them another chance. Then the whole thing started up all over again until either the victim got out or got killed. At least in this case Summer Clements had done the smart thing – got the hell out.

"She didn't want the publicity. And we have to bear that in mind. This isn't some regular person we're dealing with here. There are all kinds of other aspects to a job like this."

"Such as?" Ty asked.

"Such as making sure that she retains her dignity through all of this. And that starts with her calling the shots. Not us. You got me?"

"Still like to snap that Aussie mofo's neck."

Over Ty's shoulder, Lock could see the young actress

walking towards them. She was flanked by the head of her management team, a grey-haired man in his fifties called Frank Bernstein, and her publicist, a heavily made-up Puerto Rican woman called Paula Francis. In contrast to the bikini-clad girls draped around the pool, Summer was wearing jeans and a shirt with the name of an LA punk band, Neighborhood Watch, splashed in blood red across the front. A scarf covered any lingering bruises.

"Oh my God! What a cute dog." She bent down to pet Angel who wagged her tail and licked at Summer's hand.

Ty got some extra chairs and everyone sat down. Anywhere else in the country, the young starlet's arrival would no doubt have drawn a small flock of autograph hunters. In LA such behavior marked you out as either a tourist, or worse, as what people in the entertainment business scathingly referred to as 'a civilian.'

Introductions complete, her manager, Frank Bernstein, began the meeting. "Mr. Lock, we're very grateful that you could make yourself available. Obviously discretion's an issue for us, which is why we wanted to go with someone from out of town. And your reputation precedes you."

Lock smiled. It was cards on the table time. A couple of dead Neo-Nazis had probably cemented what people euphemistically referred to as his reputation. "We're happy to be of service," he said. "Now beyond ensuring your client's day-to-day safety, which is no doubt something that I'm sure any number of private security operators in Los Angeles could do adequately, what outcome do you want to see from us?"

Since she had sat down, Summer's fingernails had been tapping out an anxious drumbeat on the glass. Either she was on something or she was stressed.

"I want to get my friggin' life back. That's what I want," she said.

Paula the publicist reached out a comforting hand and

rested it on the actress's hand. Summer batted it away.

What some might have seen as a display of bratty petulance, Lock recognized as a young woman under incredible stress. He met Summer's gaze. "As far as your line of work allows for it, that's something we can achieve. You go about your life as you would normally and if there is a situation where you are made to feel uncomfortable in any way, or a situation where either Tyrone or I perceive a threat to your safety, then we'll deal with it."

There was something hanging in the air unresolved and Lock thought it best to get it out of the way before they went any further. "Have you given any thought to applying for a court order against Mr. Durham?"

Summer blew a stray strand of hair away from her eyes as her publicist took that one. "Summer doesn't want to be painted as a victim in this," said Paula.

Lock didn't know what other word applied to someone who'd almost been strangled to death by an asshole boyfriend but he knew what they were saying.

"Mr. Lock," said Bernstein. "This town is all about image. Right now Summer is seen as a strong young woman, a role model to other young women, someone who is in control. She doesn't drink. She doesn't take drugs. She's not only a very talented actress, she's also a consummate professional. That's why she commands the kind of money from the studios that she does. We don't want anything getting out there into the public domain to tarnish that perception, either with the public or with the people who employ her."

"I understand completely. Since the last incident, has Mr. Durham been in contact?" asked Lock.

Bernstein and Paula traded a look that said yes.

"He won't stop," said Summer. "He hasn't even left my house. That's why I'm staying here."

Lock smiled to himself. He knew there had to be a catch

when the young actress's people had offered him and Carrie Summer's Malibu beach home to stay in. They were hiring close protection but they wanted him to throw in a free eviction service.

Summer picked up on his silence. "Don't worry, I plan on staying here. Traffic from the 'Bu's a bitch. But if you could persuade him to leave."

"We can do that," said Ty.

They'd thrown him a curveball right out of the gate but it could work to his advantage, Lock thought to himself. It would give him a chance to see just what kind of asshole he was dealing with. Lock suspected that Ty was right, that a guy like Jason Durham might not be such a tough guy after all. But he wanted some first-hand knowledge before he made up his mind.

"I have some contacts at the Malibu Sheriff's Department," offered Bernstein. "I'm sure they'd be happy to accompany you."

"That's very kind of you," said Lock. "But that may just draw more attention to the situation. If we need them, we can always give them a call. Can you handle things here while I take care of it?" he asked Ty. Ty nodded a yes. Lock looked back at Summer. "Anything else?"

Paula answered for her. "Summer's at the Chateau because she has to do some press here in the morning."

There was an edge to how she said it that deepened Lock's confusion. "Makes sense."

Bernstein coughed into his hand. "It's for the movie she did with Jason," he said, lowering his voice.

Lock caught the look on Ty's face. "He's going to be here?" Ty asked.

"It's in both their contracts," said Paula.

"As I said, we don't want this current unpleasantness going public," added Bernstein.

Lock looked from the manager to the publicist and then

to the young actress. She nibbled at a nail with a trembling hand. He got to his feet. "Let me go talk to Mr. Durham for you, make sure he vacates your property and that he's on his best behavior tomorrow."

FOUR

SUMMER'S BEACH HOUSE was in the Big Rock area of Malibu. It backed directly on to the Pacific Coast Highway, or PCH as it was known by the locals. The front faced out across the Pacific. Like the rest of Malibu it was a quiet community, although a little more diverse than somewhere like the Colony with its private gated access. Here there were people who made less than a million dollars a year.

As he rounded the bend just before Big Rock, Lock passed a Malibu Sheriff Department's patrol car. It was empty, a decoy to dissuade commuters from the San Fernando Valley from speeding. The house was up ahead, just past a rack of stop lights. Summer had already provided him with a breakdown of the layout. There were two entrances on either side. They opened onto side decks, which in turn led to glass security doors and finally to doors that opened directly into the house.

Summer usually used one of the two-door double garages, opening them electronically with a clicker and driving straight in. The garage offered direct access into the ground floor of the house via two doors, one of which opened directly into the kitchen, and another that led into a large open-plan living room.

Decks wrapped around three sides of the property. The two side decks were little more than walkways. The one on the southern side had steps that led down to the beach. There was a large upstairs deck and a smaller porch-sized deck downstairs.

Lock had a clicker for the garage but the noise of the door rolling back up would alert anyone inside the house to his arrival. Neither did he want to approach via the two doors which faced PCH.

He drove past, the house on his left, turned around at the Moonshadows bar and restaurant, and parked the Range Rover a little further down. He got out and walked down to a series of steps which offered public access to the beach. He'd made sure to time his arrival for low tide. He took off his shoes and socks and went for a stroll, his plan being to access the house directly from the beach. Summer had already furnished him with the numbered code for the external glass doors and a set of keys. This way if he came face to face with the tough-guy actor it would be just the two of them.

It was a beautiful day as he strolled down the sands. A couple of people were out walking their dogs but otherwise the place was quiet. The houses sat on pylons. At high tide the Pacific would run directly under them and the beach would disappear entirely.

Sunlight shimmered across the water. On the Big Rock itself sat a dozen or so pelicans. On a smaller rocky outcrop a herd of seals caught some rays. Even the wildlife looked super relaxed out here. It wouldn't have surprised him to see them sporting sunglasses. He expected Jason to be less laid back when he found out that Lock was here to evict him.

Lock took the set of narrow wooden steps leading up to the house two at a time. Like any good intruder who wanted to go unnoticed the key was to look like you belonged there. He pulled himself up and over the gate, landing with a thud on the other side. Two sets of steps stretched up towards the house.

About one third of the way down them stood Jason. He

was wearing red board shorts and black deck shoes. His hair was wet and he had a towel draped over his shoulders. In his hand was a Smith and Wesson Colt 45.

"You've got two seconds to tell me who the hell you are and why I shouldn't blow your head off," said the actor.

FIVE

THE COLT 45 likely had a trigger pull of around six pounds. But it took a whole lot more than six pounds of pressure when there was a real living human being in your sights rather than a paper target at the other end of a firing range. Lock knew that better than most. He had pulled the trigger of a gun more than once. When the situation called for it, he had taken life. There was a better than even chance he would be called upon to do so again over the course of his career.

Jason had killed too of course; cyborgs, vampires, zombies, extra-terrestrials. Hell, just the other month, millions of people around the world had watched him, kitted out in full tactical gear, jump from a Blackhawk and rush a compound to deliver the fatal shot to Bin Laden. And he'd almost killed Summer.

Lock waited. Nothing happened. Jason stared at him. Lock stared straight back. With every second that passed the chances of Jason actually using the gun diminished.

When Lock had decided that enough seconds had gone by, he spoke. "My name is Ryan Lock. Summer asked me to come by and speak to you."

Jason eyed him warily, and didn't lower the gun. "Why didn't you just ring the bell?"

"For one, that would have decreased the likelihood of you speaking to me. Secondly, there's a paparazzi parked just down the way."

Both points were true. Directly across PCH and up the slope was a rehab center that catered to the rich and famous, which in turn meant that the paparazzi staked out this small stretch of highway hoping to long-lens some unfortunate celebrity.

Lock continued. "I didn't think this would be a conversation you'd want to have standing out there in your shorts. Or with one of your pals at the Malibu Sheriff's Department for that matter."

Framing it as a matter of image management seemed to do the trick. Jason lowered the gun. "I would have used it," he blustered. "Just as well you spoke fast."

Lock followed the diminutive actor up the stairs and through a side door into the house. A plate of half eaten sushi lay on the black granite kitchen counter top next to a jug of what looked to Lock like green algae.

Jason put the gun down and lifted the jug. "Vegetable smoothie?" he asked.

"I'll pass," said Lock.

Jason grabbed a glass from a cabinet and poured himself a tall one. He took a sip and made a face. "I'm trying to get in shape. Start shooting again in a few weeks. Action movie," he said. "You know I'm seeing Summer tomorrow. She could have spoken to me then."

"I know that. That's why I wanted to speak with you first."

The key to dealing with someone like Jason was to remember the guy had an ego the size of a planet. If Lock started barking orders at him from the get go he was more likely to become an even bigger pain in the ass. At the same time, he couldn't tip toe around him either. It would take careful handling. That was the reason he'd come without Ty, who tended to be a little too abrasive in these situations.

"So, speak," said Jason, making a face as he chugged another inch of algae.

"Look, we both know that women can be difficult, right?" said Lock. "I just got engaged. Great gal but we have our moments. In fact we broke up for a while after we first started seeing each other. Right person, wrong time, I guess."

Jason glanced at him over the lip of the glass. "Look, I'm sure you know what happened so I'm not going to lie. I shouldn't have touched her, but sometimes she really pushed my buttons."

Lock knew there would a 'but' in there somewhere. "I'm sure she did. But the fact is, you did assault her. Now she could have gone to the cops, but she didn't."

"Yeah, and why do you think that was?" Jason asked.

Lock could take a good guess at what was coming next. Jason clearly thought Summer hadn't pressed charges because she still held a candle for him. This was one part of the discussion that he couldn't afford to tiptoe around.

"She didn't file a complaint because she doesn't need that kind of publicity any more than you do. You both know how the business you're in works. Save yourself a lot of trouble. Accept that it's over," said Lock. He looked around the open plan ground floor with its floor to ceiling picture windows framing the Pacific Ocean. "She's not coming back while you're still here."

Jason sighed. His shoulders slumped. "I was going to move out today anyway. You happy now?"

"Can I have your word on that?"

"You can," said the actor.

As they shook hands, Lock noticed that the actor was standing on his tip toes to close the gap in height between them. Judging by the heels of his deck shoes he was also wearing lifts.

Gun or no gun, it was hard to be truly intimidated by a man who wore lifts. Some of the toughest guys Lock had served with in the British Royal Military Police specialist close protection unit hadn't exactly been giants. The difference was that they didn't try to compensate for it with trick shoes.

"Gone by eighteen hundred hours?" Lock prompted.

"You got it."

Lock left by one of the doors that fronted onto the highway. Outside, parked right in front of a tow away zone sign was a Nissan Altima with a long-haired white male in his early twenties sitting in the driver's seat, a camera in hand trained up the slope at the garden of the rehab center.

Lock tapped the glass and thumbed a 'get the hell out of here' at the photographer. He took off with a squeal of rubber, and Lock walked north back up PCH to the Range Rover.

He climbed in, more anxious about the situation than he had been before. Something in his gut told him that the conversation had gone far too smoothly. There had been something else that had set off alarm bells. Jason may have been chugging down a health shake but there had also been two lines of cocaine laid out on a mirror on the dining room table. If there was one thing more unpredictable than an egomaniac movie star it was a coked up egomaniac movie star who greeted visitors with a 45.

As he drove back towards West Hollywood, he called Carrie to let her know that he had secured their deluxe beachside accommodation, but not to head over without him. Then he called Ty to give him an updated situation report.

"You think he's going to be a good boy tomorrow?" Ty asked.

"He'd better be," said Lock.

SIX

TY STOOD GUARD outside one of the Chateau's twelve bungalows. Summer was the other side of the door, getting ready for the next day's press event with her publicist. Man, so far, he thought, he was loving this gig. For a start, the young actress had taken a shine to him. He could tell. It wasn't surprising either – her being surrounded by all those metrosexual movie stars all day, half of whom who probably batted for the other team. It was just a shame that she wasn't his type – too young, too skinny. Ty liked himself a woman with some meat on her bones. He only hoped she didn't make too much of a play for him. He'd let her down gently if it came to that. Wasn't anything worth worrying about anyhow, not when he had a real worry.

It had turned out that there was a 'no firearms' rule on this gig. The LAPD were pretty strict about carry permits, either open or concealed, and Lock didn't want to fall foul of them, so for this job they would have to get by without a gun, which sucked. Ty always felt naked without his SIG Sauer.

From nowhere, Ty caught the sweet smell of dope smoke on the air. He closed his eyes for a moment, breathing in the aroma. Maybe he should just relax and enjoy the ride, he told himself.

"Wake the hell up, asshole."

His eyes snapped open to the sight of Lock glaring at him.

"Just taking a moment. She's safe inside," said Ty.

Lock glared at him. "Okay, I'm going to do a quick recon of the room they're using for the press interviews then I'm going to check that he's out of the Malibu house and pick up Carrie. Can I count on you to stay awake while I'm gone?"

"I was resting my eyes. Anyway, what's this guy gonna do if he shows up?"

"Well, he pulled a piece on me when I met him."

Ty chewed this news over slowly. "Told you we needed to be armed."

"Not gonna happen, Tyrone. But let's not just assume this is going to be a slam dunk. The guy's unpredictable and I don't like him."

"No shit. You don't like anyone," Ty said.

"Okay, I particularly don't like him," said Lock.

Lock was always sweating stuff. "She's heading off to shoot another movie soon, and you said he was too. All we have to do is get her through tomorrow."

"And tonight," said Lock.

"Chill, brother. I'm on it." Ty held out his fist and they bumped.

Two bikini-clad model types weaved around Ty on their way to one of the other bungalows. He made sure not to even glance in their direction. Man, he wished Lock would let him wear his shades.

SEVEN

BY THE TIME Lock got back to Malibu all traces of the actor were gone – Jason had been as good as his word. The remote clicker for the garage and his set of keys sat on the marble countertop of the bar which fronted onto the living area, along with a brief note for Summer, apologizing once again for his behavior. Lock picked up the keys and clicker and left the note where it was. He was tempted to throw it into the trash but it was rarely a good idea to interfere in personal matters.

He would advise Summer that she should have all the locks changed in case Jason had either cloned the garage door opener or copied the keys. Lock did a careful walk through of the property, paying particular attention to any possible traces of drugs. He wouldn't have put it past Jason to leave behind a bunch of blow and put in a call to the Sheriff's department himself so that he could get even with his now ex-girlfriend.

Once Lock was satisfied that the house was it should be, he called Carrie, arranging to meet her for dinner before they headed back. The tide was in and Lock could hear heavy stones, washed smooth by the ocean, crashing into the pylons that supported the house. It was an ominous sound.

He had dinner with Carrie at a roadside Thai joint just north of the turn that led up into Topanga Canyon. With the main business of the day settled, Lock could relax. Carrie looked stunning. They held hands under the table like a couple of teenagers and Carrie teased Lock about his lack of dexterity when it came to using chopsticks. Inevitably, the conversation turned to work.

"So what's the deal with Jason?" Carrie asked him as the waitress cleared their plates.

"The bad news is that he's your standard Hollywood alpha male asshole with a drug problem and a bad attitude when it comes to women. The good news is that I think she got a real scare when he tried to strangle her. I don't think that she'll be going back for more."

"I'll drink to that," said Carrie, lifting her glass of white wine and clinking it against Lock's glass of water.

"Me too," said Lock.

They had both seen enough of life to know that Summer was one of the lucky ones. Domestic violence was like a frog being boiled slowly in a pan of water. By the time the abused partner realized how hot it was, it was often too late to climb out.

They paid for their meal and headed back to the beach house. "This is some place," said Carrie as they walked in.

She took his hand and started to lead him up the stairs. "Wonder what the view's like from the bedroom?" she said as he followed her.

Halfway up the stairs his cell phone rang. It was Ty. Carrie sighed in frustration.

"What's up?" Lock asked his partner.

"We got ourselves a situation," said Ty.

"Jason showed up?" guessed Lock.

"No, that I could deal with. It's the principal."

EIGHT

LOCK CAUGHT UP with Ty outside the bungalow. "She's freaking out," said Ty.

"Freaking out how?" he asked him.

"One minute she was talking to that chick Paula, all nice and calm. Next thing I know, she saying she's too scared to face the media tomorrow and Paula is telling her that it's in her contract and that she has to do it." Ty lowered his voice. "She's scared. I'm sorry, man, I know you were having some down time but I don't deal well with stuff like this."

Lock clapped Ty on the shoulder. "You mean like emotions?"

"Yeah, all that feelings shit and stuff. Not my area."

"Don't worry. I'll talk to her. Has she had any phone calls from him? Emails? A text?" Lock asked.

That was the problem with the plethora of modern communications. Someone could exit an abusive relationship and yet still be subjected to abuse via a host of other channels. Sure, people could be blocked on Facebook and Twitter but abusive former partners, not to mention anonymous trolls, were often skilled at working around online safeguards. It made Lock wonder why so many kids craved fame when the downside was so vast. Wealthy clients he had worked for knew that, often paying substantial sums to make sure that their names never appeared in the gossip columns. Showbiz was different though. You traded privacy not for fame but for money, but like every trade there was a price on the other end. Once you stepped over that line it was difficult to step back again.

Ty took a moment to consider Lock's question. "I asked but she said she'd already switched cell numbers, and her social media is all handled by her management. She doesn't even look at any of it," Ty said.

"Smart girl," said Lock, "I'll speak to her." He moved past Ty and knocked at the bungalow door. After a while it opened a crack and Paula, the PR woman, peeked out. "Can I come in?" Lock asked her.

She opened the door. He walked in. Summer was perched on the couch, her head in her hands. Her face was a mask of smeared make-up and long tangled red hair. She clasped a mascara-stained tissue clasped in her right hand.

"I'm sorry," she said. "You were supposed to be spending the evening with your fiancee, right?"

"Don't apologize," he said. "You mind if I sit down?"

She scooted along the couch a little. He shot the PR lady his best 'gimme a minute here' look and she disappeared into one of the bedrooms. He sat next to Summer and let the moment settle. There was an end table with a box of lavender-scented tissues. He plucked one out and handed it to her.

"Here," he said, taking the damp tissue she was holding in trade. He threw it across the room at a small trash container next to a desk. It bounced off the edge and fell onto the carpet. He left it where it was.

"You really suck at that," she said.

"Ty's the basketball player," he said. "But I am good at keeping people safe. I promise you nothing's going to happen to you while I'm here."

"And what if it already has?"

Without having to ask, he knew what she was talking about. Abuse and the damage it caused took many forms.

Perhaps the deepest and most difficult to heal was psychological. He didn't have to be a shrink to see that Summer's relationship with Jason had wounded her in ways that went way beyond the physical. Over the years he had seen people with amazing physical resilience and mental strength crumble when confronted with situations they found traumatic. When you had one view of how the world worked, only to discover a colder, more hostile reality, the realization could leave its mark. Whether it was watching a child being blow sky high on the streets of Kabul or having someone you loved and trusted try to strangle the life out of you with his bare hands, a shadow was left behind.

"Hey," said Lock. "You don't have to do anything you don't want to. That's rule number one."

She stared at the carpet. "Try telling the studio that."

"The hell with them. You really think they'd go after you for breach of contract under the circumstances?"

"No." The word came in a whisper.

He was getting through to her. Whether she did or didn't do the press in the morning was immaterial to him. What was important was that she understood she wasn't being pressured or guilt-tripped into doing it. The poor kid had likely experienced enough of that to last a lifetime from her ex-boyfriend.

"You don't know what it's like," said Summer. "Everybody sees all this," she swept a hand out, taking in the opulence of the room. "And they think that someone like me can't have any problems." She looked back to Lock. "Do you know what's it like not to be able to trust anybody?"

Lock thought back to his recent sojourn undercover in Pelican Bay Supermax, a place so racially divided and full of intrigue that to even talk to someone with different color skin was tantamount to asking for a death sentence. "I've been in difficult situations before, but no I don't know what it's like to live the life you have."

"My whole life," she said, "I've been judged by people who don't even know me but think they do. As soon as I walked into a casting I was either too short, too tall, too young looking, too old. Then when you do manage to build a career for yourself, it just gets worse. You wake up one day and you're surrounded by people kissing your ass but you know that the only reason they're doing it is because they want something from you. It's tiring, you know. Everything I wear, everything I say. I gain five pounds, and I'm front page of the Enquirer."

Lock didn't say anything. It was good that she was confiding in him. He had to have trust for this to work.

"That was why I liked Jason," she went on. "He'd been through it all. He knew the game. He knew that it was a game. I didn't have to pretend to be someone I wasn't with him." Her eyes began to fill again with tears. "But he wanted something from me too. In the end, he was the same as everyone else."

"So why do it at all? Why not walk away?" he asked, his curiosity genuine.

"Why do you keep doing what you do, Mr. Lock?"

Lock smiled. Like most people he didn't give too much day to day thought to his choice of profession. You got up. You went to work. You came home.

"I guess that I do this because I enjoy it and it's what I'm good at."

"Same for me with acting. When I'm in rehearsals or on set, I'm all good. It's the other stuff that's hard."

Something occurred to Lock. "I protect people and you act. So go in there tomorrow and act like you're cool with everything. Pretending. That's what your job boils down to, right?"

"I guess."

"So tomorrow let's both do that."

She swallowed. He could see some small measure of

composure return to her. She sat up a little straighter. "You'll be with me?"

Lock fixed her with his eyes. "Every step. If he even so much as looks at you the wrong way, I'll really give the reporters something to write about."

NINE

LOCK WALKED OUT of the bungalow to where Ty was standing. "I'm going to take another look at the room they're using tomorrow then I'll be back and you can go rest."

"She okay?"

"For now."

He left Ty and walked down the path to the swimming pool. A scattering of people sat at tables, most of them smokers, refugees from the hotel bar. A couple of movie executive types, suit jackets slung over the back of chairs, shirts unbuttoned, puffed on cigars the size of small torpedoes. At the next table Lock recognized a very famous male actor with old-school matinee idol good looks who was always being pictured with a dazzling array of beautiful women. He was holding hands under the table with another man.

A little further back, safe from the reflection of the pool lights, sat a lone male. He was nursing a whisky and smoking a cigarette, his face shadowed by a hat. He looked up at Lock and smiled.

Lock walked over to the table, and Jason gestured for him to sit down. "What are you doing here?" Lock asked.

Maybe it was the booze, or just what Summer had already seen, but there was a malevolence in Jason's eyes, a bitterness to his expression that had been absent at the beach house.

"You kicked me out of the place I was staying, remember? I have press here in the morning, and besides," he slurred, lifting his crystal tumbler of Scotch, "the bar here's pretty good. But don't worry, bodyguard, I'm not going to cause any trouble."

Lock kept himself calm and his voice even. Jason was a man spoiling for a fight and Lock rolling around poolside with him would do no one any favors, least of all Summer who had only just gotten herself together and whose bungalow was within earshot of any potential disturbance.

"I didn't think you would," said Lock, getting up.

"You want a drink?" Jason asked, the hatred in his eyes at odds with the drunken grin plastered over his face.

"I'm on duty."

Jason laughed. "Very professional of you."

Lock started to walk away without reply.

"She's a great lay. If you or your buddy get a shot at her, take it," Jason shouted after him, loud enough to draw glances from the other people around the pool.

It would have been the easiest thing in the world for Lock to turn on his heel, walk back to the table, and obliterate the loud-mouthed Aussie. But it would have achieved the square root of zero. For Lock, violence was like a lot like Jason – just a tool.

He kept walking, taking the long way round as he headed back to the bungalow. He pulled Ty one to one side, careful to keep his voice to a whisper.

Ty glared in the direction of the pool as Lock brought him up to speed.

"So what's the play if he shows up?" Ty asked.

"Kick his ass then call the cops," said Lock. "In that order."

TEN

SAVE FOR A couple of gelled lights arranged to make the two stars of the movie look their best in front of the single camera, the room was dark. Lock watched from a position off to one side as a fresh-faced Summer walked into the room with Ty. He was starting to see why she made the big bucks. Even as she took her seat next to a grizzled Jason, who was still clearly suffering the after-effects of last night's one-man whisky party, there was no hint that she was anything other than happy and relaxed.

The two stars were seated in old-fashioned canvas director chairs that had their names on the back. Much to Lock's amusement, the legs of Jason's chair appeared to be three of four inches longer than Summer's. With the cameraman shooting them from the waist up it would make Jason appear to be the taller of two. A huge red and black one-sheet for the movie was positioned directly behind them, the two stars looking brooding and serious as they stared at each other across the poster, no doubt focused on a possible Oscar nomination.

The drill was standard for these types of events. Members of the US and overseas press corps who covered Hollywood and related entertainment news would have fifteen minutes each with the two stars. Five minutes with Jason, five with Summer, and five minutes of joint interview questions. The questions were standard, and so, Lock realized after the first few interviews, were the answers. It was mind numbing to watch.

Jason palmed a couple of painkillers with some coffee as the third joint interview ended. He only spoke to Summer when a reporter was present and lapsed back into a sullen silence when it was just them and the attendant cameraman, PR people, Lock, and Ty. Even if he had wanted a fight, he didn't look like he would be able to summon the energy. Lock was relieved. There were only six more hours to go. After that the only time Summer would have to deal with this douchebag would be a chance encounter at a party or awards ceremony.

As the morning wore on, the questions remained as turgid but the young actress's mood seemed to lift. It was an ordeal but one with an end in sight. They broke for lunch early – around noon – and Summer retreated back to her bungalow, escorted at a discrete distance by both Lock and Ty.

"So far, so good," said Ty.

Even Lock, who for professional reasons always tried to anticipate a worst case scenario, had to agree. "Yup. He seems to have settled down."

A day or so later Summer would be on a plane, heading for the set of her next movie. Lock and Ty would have banked a hefty sum and the young actress, grateful for Lock's support, both practical and emotional, had already said he and Carrie could stay in the Malibu beach house until they had to return to New York. As close protection jobs went it had been easy money.

After lunch, Jason bounced back into the room. He made a beeline for Lock. Lock guessed that lunch had probably consisted of a couple of lines of cocaine and a couple of beers to settle his stomach.

Jason stuck out his hand. "Listen, mate, I really am sorry about last night. Dunno what got into me. Are we good?"

Lock stared at him with dead eyes until the actor dropped his hand back down by his side. "Okay, mate, I don't blame you for not wanting to shake. No worries."

He skulked back to his seat as Summer came back into the room and took her position. Jason smiled broadly at her. "You look great."

He reached over to touch her knee and from the corner of the room Ty made a noise that sounded to Lock distinctly like a growl.

"Touch her anywhere, little man, and I'll chop your goddamn hand off and feed it to you," said the six foot four former Marine.

The respective PR people started to look flustered. "We have Deadline Hollywood next, so if everyone could settle down," said Jason's PR person.

Jason open-palmed another apology. "Relax, folks, we're all good. I was just being friendly."

"Let's just get this done," said Summer, some of her previous poise evaporating.

The remains of the afternoon dragged for everyone besides Jason who took a bathroom break after an hour, returning even more manic than before. He had presumably refreshed himself with some more Bolivian marching powder. Twice, Lock had to speak to him out of earshot of reporters. Both times Jason apologized. He was clearly testing the boundaries, a toddler trapped in a man's body.

Around five thirty in the afternoon, the final reporter was escorted in. A hyperactive Jason shifted in his chair, animated and cracking jokes. Summer did her best to match his mood but Lock could see her wilting from the stress of the situation. It had been a long day.

Having waxed lyrical about the movie, the reporter asked his final question. "So when are we going to see you two back on screen together?"

Summer was first to answer. "Well, I really enjoyed working with such a talented actor. I guess it all depends on the right project coming up."

The reporter nodded. It had already been explained that questions about their relationship were off-limits and the one or two journalists who had edged in that direction had been very firmly guided back to the movie by the PR handlers.

Jason smiled broadly when it came his turn. He dug into his pocket for his cell phone, and fiddled with the display as he answered the question.

"I don't know, Bob," he said to the reporter. "Summer is a very exciting performer. The public just might be surprised. The world may be seeing us together on screen sooner than everyone thinks."

At this, Summer was up and out of her chair with a hurried, "Sorry, I don't feel well. I think it's the lights," to the reporter as she hightailed it from the room. Lock nodded for Ty to go with her.

Jason looked over at Lock and grinned. Lock stayed in neutral. He knew that Jason wanted a reaction for two reasons. For one, if Lock did hit him, the level of violence would be constrained by the presence of the camera and the other people present. Second, any reaction by Lock would have negative implications for Summer.

What they had now was a grade-A Hollywood asshole conforming to type. It was hardly news and containable. The reporter would be spoken to, that section of the footage, which was being shot on the distributor's dime, would be scrubbed. There would be no story.

"Nice try," Lock said to Jason whose grin had faded as everyone in the room stared at him.

ELEVEN

LOCK AND TY sat together in the living area of Summer's bungalow. Through the closed bedroom door they could hear her choked sobs. It had taken the best part of an hour for them to work out precisely why the young actress had reacted so violently to Jason's comments.

Ty held up a smartphone, tilting the screen so Lock could see it. It was full-screened to the video player. On the screen was a close up of Summer's face as it had appeared in movie theaters around the world. But this time the image was grainy and badly lit. In the background Lock recognized the master bedroom of Summer's Malibu beach house; the foot of the bed, a dressing table, a mirror that threw back the reflection of Jason holding up a cell phone in one hand and an unwrapped condom in the other.

"You wanna play?" he said.

On screen, Summer smiled at him, pushing herself up the bed and revealing her bare breasts.

"You can kill that," said Lock.

Ty tapped the screen and the image disappeared.

Since One Night in Paris, the homemade sex tape which had catapulted Paris Hilton into the public eye, celebrity sex tapes had become a sad feature of a tawdry cultural landscape where absolutely nothing was sacred. At first they had been leaked to the media, or online, as a way of boosting a celebrity's public profile. But over the past few years, with the growth of camera phones, YouTube, and social networking sites, they had increasingly been used by men seeking to humiliate and even blackmail former partners.

"He emailed it to her?" Lock asked Ty.

Ty nodded. "She had her cell phone switched off during the interview. She switched it back on after she left the room and there it was. Time stamp says he sent it around lunchtime. This was what he was talking about when he started talking shit back there."

Lock chewed at his lip for a second. "Any message?"

"Just some bull about remembering the good times. He was pretty careful about how he worded it," said Ty.

"Yeah, the guy has a real way with words," Lock said, knowing that if Jason had hinted at anything else they could have him arrested for blackmail.

"What we gonna do?" Ty said.

"I'm going to call Carrie," said Lock. "Get her take on this."

"Best not mention that to Summer's people," Ty said, with a nod towards the bedroom door.

Although Carrie was a reporter, she and Lock had a deal that they could both discuss their working lives without it going any further unless they were both cool with it. She had never let him down and he couldn't see a situation where she would.

Lock headed back to the Range Rover to make the call, doubly aware of how sensitive it was. Carrie answered on the third buzz.

"Hey, cowboy. You all done?" Carrie said.

She sounded relaxed and happy. In the background he could hear Angel barking, the surf rolling in on the beach below and the squawk of a seagull who had taken to hanging out on the deck.

"Not quite."

He gave Carrie a brief summary.

"Has it leaked yet?" she asked him once he had finished.

"Not yet, but it looks like it's just a matter of time. The guy's pretty unstable."

"What are her management and PR people saying?"

"Difficult to get any sense out of them," Lock told her. "They're freaked too. I mean she doesn't want something as private as this broadcast all over the internet. It's not like she's some reality TV star. The kid has a major league acting career in front of her. Might be good publicity if you're looking for fifteen minutes but she's in the game for the long haul."

Carrie sighed. "You know once it's out there that's it. TMZ or someone picks it up first, then the tabloids, and then the mainstream media run with it. Meanwhile it's gone viral and there's no way of putting the genie back in the bottle."

"So what you're telling me is I can't save her from this?" Lock said.

"Not unless you can get hold of the footage and persuade him to destroy it."

"I'm not exactly his favorite person."

They were at a dead end. It only took the click of a button to cause someone untold misery these days and Jason's finger was right over that button. If Lock didn't find a way to stop this fiasco in its tracks he would have failed his principal. There was physical damage. There was emotional damage. Then there was reputational damage. Sometimes it was easier to make a recovery from the first than the other two. When he took on the job of protecting someone it went far beyond making sure they weren't physically harmed. He was responsible for all aspects of their well being.

Lock had watched the tabloid exposure of various celebrities down the years where they were held up to public ridicule for no other reason than it made someone money. He wasn't about to allow something like that to happen to someone he worked for. He didn't know how he would stop it, but he would find a way, and if he couldn't then he would make sure that Jason paid a heavy price. That was the deal with Lock. If he was on your side, he was on your side until the job was done.

TWELVE

LOCK SAT WITH his bare feet dangling over the edge of the Chateau's swimming pool as Ty came out to check on him. It was past two in the morning. Ty slipped off his sneakers and socks and sat down beside him. Both men stared for a while at the shimmering blue water.

"How's Summer?" Lock asked.

"Sleeping," said Ty.

They lapsed back into silence. Ty was worried. Not for his friend and partner —but for Jason. When Lock went quiet and descended into a brooding silence was when you had to watch out. His eyes were hooded. He didn't smile. There was a darkness to him that swept outwards to take in everything in his orbit.

"You know if we mess this guy up everyone's going to know it was you. Could be bad."

Lock shot him a sideways glance. "Don't worry. I got something way more satisfying in mind."

"Like what?" asked Ty

"You'll see," said Lock.

"Just don't be asking me to make a sex tape with the dude. Movie star or not, I don't roll in that direction."

"Which is probably a huge relief to the entire gay community," Lock said. He took a breath. "Everyone's got a weak spot, even someone like Jason. What do you think keeps him up at night? Apart from booze and blow. What do you think he fears the most?"

Ty shrugged. "Breaking a nail? The hell if I know."

"Think about it, Tyrone. He's an actor, a tough-guy movie star, the man runs on ego. If he was made of chocolate he'd eat himself. What would kill him inside?"

"I still don't know," said Ty, frustrated.

"Well, I'm going to show you. But it's going to take some work and Summer's cooperation. I think I can talk her round to it but I'll need you to hire the logistics."

"Just tell me what you need."

Lock pulled out a single sheet of lined paper, unfolded it and handed it to Ty. "My list of requirements."

Ty scanned the list and a broad grin formed. "Oh, you bad, Lock. You real bad."

THIRTEEN

THE LOS ANGELES Police Department tended to stay out of celebrity spats until there was an actual criminal offense, or the clearly evidenced threat of one. It was a solid policy and one Lock would have followed had he been in their position. They had a force of ten thousand officers and an urban population of almost four million people that left them straining to deal with the major crimes that occurred daily – armed robbery, homicides, rapes, murder-suicides, kidnappings, and the ever present threat of a terrorist attack. An ex-boyfriend refusing to hand over footage of his girlfriend performing a sex act on him wasn't up there. But their understandable indifference cut both ways. As long as Lock was careful, they wouldn't be looking too carefully at him working on a little bit of payback.

Lock handed Ty two thousand dollars in cash and sent him off to begin preparations. Cash would ensure that there was no trail back to them. He had also given Ty the name of a location scout he'd gotten from Summer's manager. The job of a location scout in the movie business was fairly self explanatory but more broadly they were fixers, able to arrange access to places and have those places secured sufficiently that a production crew could film without interruption, which was precisely what Lock's plan called for.

The next part required Summer's assistance. When he sat

down and outlined what he had in mind and what he wanted her to do for him she was nervous. Like many people in her situation she wanted the whole problem to just disappear into thin air. He explained to her that wasn't going to happen.

"Listen to me," said Lock. "He will leak that footage. Maybe not today or tomorrow but at some point. Or he's going to hold it over you and you're not going to get a good night's sleep while he does."

Summer looked around nervously. "Couldn't you just, I dunno, beat him up or something?"

"I'd be breaking the law."

"But if there were no witnesses..." she went on.

In truth, Lock had already considered the possibility more than once by now. "Me doing that might make you feel better. Hell, it would make me feel better. I'd enjoy it. I know Ty would love the opportunity to kick his ass. But there's a problem when you ask someone like us to give someone a beating." Lock paused. He wanted what he was going to say next to sink in. "Maybe he has a heart condition that no one knows about? Or we land a blow in the wrong place or too hard? Then the guy's dead. Would you be prepared to live with that?" he asked.

She shook her head. "Of course not."

"I'm glad to hear it. And even if we just slapped him around a little, he'd still be all the more likely to release the tape because his ego would have been wounded. That would put you right back to square one. So what I'm suggesting is something a little more long term. This is like the Cold War. Russia didn't bomb us because they knew that we'd wipe them out. Mutually assured destruction. Now he's got his nuke and we need one of our own. When that's in place then we cut the deal."

Summer blew a stray strand of hair from her eyes as he laid out what he wanted her to do.

Lock nodded. "At the place I mentioned. You said you'd

been there with him before?"

When he had finished, she said, "Sounds simple."

"The best plans usually are," said Lock.

She pulled her cell phone from her bag, and clicked down her contacts list. She pulled up Jason's number and hit the call button on the screen. Lock could see the tremble in her hands.

"Jason, hi. It's me."

Lock had installed an app on her phone that allowed calls to be recorded. A separate split jack meant that he could listen in, even though he already knew how it would play. Men like Jason lived for the game. More than anything else they cherished their ability to get into someone's head and stay there. That was why, when a woman decided to truly sever all ties with an abusive partner, they often reacted violently. They could deal with everything except being ignored.

Jason's suspicion quickly gave way. Summer didn't seek to reconcile first. Instead she expressed her worry about the footage and whether anyone else had seen it. Jason said they hadn't. Summer's relief was genuine.

"Thank you," she said to her ex, no doubt hating herself as she said it. Lock gave her a thumbs up. He would run the recording through voice analysis software after the call and be able to know for sure whether Jason was telling the truth about having shared the sex tape.

The offer of a truce prompted a small measure of contrition on Jason's part. He made the request to meet her. Without giving a clear no, she played hard to get, finally agreeing but insisting on setting the time and location and hanging up before he had a chance to try to take things in a different direction.

Mission accomplished. They had Jason where they wanted him, and best of all, he probably thought it was all his idea.

FOURTEEN

DINNER WAS SET for nine o' clock. Nine was late by Hollywood standards, where a pile of spec scripts or book galleys usually demanded early nights. The restaurant was a small Indian place on Westwood Boulevard not too far from UCLA. Summer would arrive alone.

Lock and Ty would stay out of sight. They had weighed the risks and felt that Jason was unlikely to do anything in public but if he sensed their presence or even caught so much as a glimpse of them he would be gone and their chance to lift the weight of the footage from Summer's shoulders would have slipped.

They had given the young actress a crash course in self defense. Don't throw a punch. Hit with your elbows and knees – the hardest parts of your body. Aim for the weak spots; groin, throat, eyes, solar plexus. As soon as you have the chance to run, take it. It was all pretty much common sense, though in Lock's experience, common sense wasn't all that common.

Carrie had spent the day on the phone working her contacts. The news was mixed. Lots of people now seemed to know about the sex tape, a few of the sleazier ones were sniffing around the story, but so far Jason was neither confirming or denying its existence. It wasn't out there. That could change with the click of a send button – and with that click or tap of a screen would come a world of pain for

Lock's principal.

At the wheel of the black Range Rover, Lock drove north on Westwood Boulevard staying a block behind Summer's Prius. Carrie had already found street parking opposite the small Indian restaurant where Summer was due to meet Jason. The choice of location had been crucial. Somewhere like Westwood or Century City was where celebrities went if they didn't want to run the gauntlet of paparazzi who hung out in West Hollywood, Beverly Hills, and along the Sunset Strip. Westwood was more business district than residential and that meant the type of location they had been looking for was easier to find here.

As instructed, Summer hung a right into a ten storey parking structure a block from the restaurant. Lock dropped back into traffic, disappearing into a red sea of brake lights. He keyed his radio. For this operation, they had ditched their cell phones back at the beach house with Angel as they didn't want calls between them being traced. As far as the cellular networks were concerned everyone, apart from Summer, was sitting in Malibu.

"Ty?" said Lock.

"Yes, sir."

"You have a visual?"

"Sure do."

"Okay, let me know when she's on the way back down and you can confirm the vehicle location."

"Will do."

Lock turned into a side street, drove down it a few hundred yards, one-eightied the Range Rover and stopped.

His radio crackled. "I have her. She's walking out," said Ty.

"Thanks," said Lock.

There was another burst of static and then Carrie came on. "He just arrived."

"Anyone with him?" Lock asked.

"No, he's alone. He valet parked and walked straight in. Okay, I have her at the corner of Westwood and Kinross. She's a couple of minutes away."

"Let me know when they're both inside," said Lock.

Three minutes later Carrie confirmed that Summer and Jason were both inside the restaurant. Carrie would stay where she was. As soon as they left the restaurant, Carrie would have eyes on them again.

Lock pulled away from the sidewalk and tracked back to the parking structure where Summer had left her Prius.

The Range Rover turned into the concrete high rise parking garage. There were two lanes for traffic coming in and two lanes for traffic coming out. You picked up your ticket from a machine on the way in. The first twenty minutes were free, after that there was an hourly charge. The opening hours were six in the morning until midnight. On the way out you paid at one of several pay stations on each of the garage's ten levels. There were two stairwells, one at the east and one at the west end of the structure. The west facing stairwell also had an elevator.

Lock stopped at the ticket machine closest to the glass-fronted attendant's booth. He glanced over at the attendant who was decked out in a blue uniform that made him look like a cross between a minor league baseball player and a video game Mario Brother. The attendant was busy studying a rack of closed circuit display screens, his face obscured by a matching blue ball cap that was pulled down low over his eyes.

The attendant looked up and glared at Lock. He had to choke back a laugh as Ty ran his finger around the collar of his blue parking attendant shirt. He scowled as he slid open the glass window of the booth. "We got a problem with the top three levels so they're closed. Other than that, park where you like," said Ty.

Lock strained to read Ty's name badge. "Thanks for the heads up, Miguel," he said, pressing the button and waiting for a ticket. The screen embedded into the machine that would usually have displayed a live video feed of his Range Rover was blank.

Ty muttered something Lock didn't quite catch, and slammed the window back shut.

Lock worked his way up to level seven before running into a series of bright orange cones. A chain strung across the ramp blocked any further progress. He pulled into a spot at the end of a row next to a double cab Dodge Ram. According to the parking attendant Ty had paid three hundred dollars to take the day off, the truck had been there for three days. Lock got out, ducked under the chain and walked up the rest of the way, the levels eerily empty.

The only car on the top level was Summer's Toyota Prius. It was parked in the very middle of a row of spaces that faced out onto the windowless back wall of an office building. A concrete lip rose about three feet. Beyond the lip was a sheer drop to an alleyway.

Lock glanced up to check out the brand new HD quality surveillance camera that had been installed specially to capture a twenty by twenty area. Behind him were another two cameras, triangulating the area around Summer's car. Each camera fed back directly, via an encrypted Wi-Fi connection, to a central server. They also had memory cards in case the Wi-Fi connection was lost. The cameras themselves were housed in the type of reinforced casing that you would find in a million other public places. He could have gone for smaller cameras but had elected for hiding them in plain sight. People were so used to cameras watching them these days that they barely even registered, and certainly not when the individual was in a pressurized situation.

He keyed his radio. "You have a visual?"

"You're all set for your close-up, brother," came Ty's reply.

FIFTEEN

SUMMER FOLDED HER napkin over her lap and kept her hands there. That way Jason couldn't see how much she was shaking. He was all smiles and small talk as they ordered, a star-struck waiter fluttering around them until finally Jason asked him to give them some privacy.

Jason looked down at her plate – the food untouched. "Not hungry?"

She shrugged. "Can we talk about the video you sent me?"

He chewed a mouthful of Bhaji, his eyes never leaving her face. "What video?" he said, his mouth still half full.

"Let's not play games here."

He smirked. "You used to like games. Remember that game where I used to tie you up. Or the one where..."

"The video," she said. It felt like everyone in the restaurant was staring at her, that they'd heard. She imagined that if tonight didn't work, this would be what the rest of her life would feel like. People watching. Of course Jason would be some kind of stud and she would be relegated to that all too common Hollywood role - the whore.

"Okay, okay. The video," Jason said. He waved the waiter over and ordered another Kingfisher beer. "Good times, huh?" he said to her. "Good times."

"I want you to destroy it."

He took a sip of beer and made a sighing noise. "You

want some of this?" he asked her.

It was as much as she could do not to pick up the glass and throw it over him. "No, thank you."

She had to remain calm. Lock had impressed that on her. The chances were that Jason wasn't going to change his spots and do the decent thing. They had to give him the opportunity first though. When he refused then they would go to plan B. Lock's note on that had been simple too. Get Jason into position but don't make it too obvious. Improvise if you had to. Lock would have made a good director she'd thought as he'd run through his solution.

"Okay, so say for sake of argument that I have this video you're talking about. It's all I have left to remember you by. I mean memories fade but something like that, well it's a little more permanent."

She could see his enjoyment of her discomfort etched on his face. He was getting off on it. She did her best to re-focus. This was a scene like any other.

"If you still have any feelings for me, Jason..."

It was his turn to cut her off. "Oh, that's precious. What about me, huh? You've been going round telling half the town I'm some kind of psycho."

She couldn't bring herself to let this go. He was a psycho and it wasn't news. "You could have killed me."

"Jesus, don't be so melodramatic," he said, pounding the rest of his beer and waving for another before the empty glass had touched back down on the table. It was his fourth since he had arrived.

"It's the truth," she said, trying to regroup. He wasn't going to concede anything, not unless he was forced into it. She would give it one last try but that was it. "Please, Jason. I'm begging you. I don't want this hanging over me."

Carrie sat across the street, listening to the conversation taking place inside the restaurant. She keyed her radio.

"Lock?"

"I'm here."

"He's not going for it," she said.

"Didn't think he would," he replied. "Let me know when they leave."

Back inside the restaurant, Summer had shifted gears. Now it was all about plan B and that required a transition.

First she ordered a drink from the waiter. The request met with Jason's approval.

"That's my girl," he said. "You are way too uptight these days. You really have to learn to loosen up."

"You want something to remember me by?" she said. "How about one last time? For old time's sake."

Across the table his smile rearranged itself into a leer. She knew she could rely on his baser instincts.

"Now you're talking," Jason said. "You missed me, right? That's what all this has been about."

She giggled. "You know me better than I know myself. So what do you say? Shall we..."

Jason was already waving for the check.

SIXTEEN

IT WAS KNOWN in the close protection trade as a come on – a pre-arranged decoy or distraction that served as a prelude to the main event. It could take many forms; a vocal protestor rushing past a barricade, drawing a bodyguard away from their principal and making the real assassin's job that much easier; a small IED designed to cause injury which drew the rescuers into the kill zone of a much larger device. The come on had many variations but none was simpler or more effective than a man being led by his baser instincts into a bad situation – in this case, a deserted parking structure.

Lock listened to Carrie's updates in his earpiece as Summer walked Jason back to the Prius. He risked a smile. This was like shooting fish in a barrel.

Down in the parking attendant's booth, Ty watched as the couple walked towards the elevator. The elevator route had been selected to ensure that Jason wouldn't see the closed off, empty parking levels until it was too late.

Summer pushed the call button. Ty kept his head down but he needn't have worried. Jason was way too wrapped up in the young actress to notice him. For most people in a big city, parking attendants, even those of the six foot four variety, were so much urban foliage.

Jason pawed at the actress, and the doors closed. Ty

couldn't wait to see the asshole's expression when he stepped out on the top floor to be greeted by Lock. It was payback time and the Australian actor had earned everything that was coming his way.

Ty waited for the call light to disappear. He keyed his radio. "On their way."

Twenty four seconds. That was the time it would take the elevator to make its way up to the top floor. Lock had timed it – twice. He checked his watch, counting the seconds. He began moving into position so that he wouldn't be visible when the elevator doors opened.

As the second hand of his watch swept down towards the twenty four second mark, he tensed, ready to make his move. The elevator doors didn't open. Twenty five seconds. Twenty six. He listened hard for the whine of the cable or the whir of the motor but the only noise was the distant sound of traffic from Westwood Boulevard.

SEVENTEEN

JASON HAD HER backed into the corner of the elevator. His right hand ran up her thigh. She could smell the beer on his breath as he whispered into her ear. "Why don't we just do it here?...You'd like that, right?....Couldn't stay away from me, could you?" On and on he went, his erotic monologue making her stomach lurch as he pawed at her.

She could see the control panel where he had pulled out the stop button. She had no way of reaching it from where she was. They were between floors. Unless there was an override it would be impossible for either Lock or Ty to get to her. And even if they could it would blow the element of surprise that they needed.

She tried to dredge up what she'd been taught about self defense. He was so close to her that she could barely move. Her back was against the side panel. She needed to get some distance between them.

"Hold on there," she whispered to him, desperately trying to keep the panic out of her voice. "Let me take my jeans off."

He took a step back. She put her arms on his shoulders and ran her tongue over her lips. He smiled with anticipation and closed his eyes.

Her hands tightened on his shoulders. She brought her right knee up as hard as she could into his groin.

He roared with pain as her knee slammed into his groin.

She let go of him and scrambled towards the elevator panel. She hit the plunger of the emergency stop button back into place and jabbed a finger at the already lit level ten. The elevator shuddered back into life.

Jason was still doubled over.

The elevator inched upwards as he staggered towards her. "You bitch, I'm going to fucking kill you for that," said Jason, advancing on her. "No," said Jason. "I got an even better idea. I'm going to make sure the world knows what a little slut you truly are."

She was backed against the doors now. As they began to open, she fell backwards. Jason loomed over her, ready to pounce, his fists clenched.

A car appeared from nowhere and the passenger door opened. A blonde woman leaned over. "Get in," she said. Summer didn't need to be asked twice. She climbed into the passenger seat. The car took off at speed before she had even closed the door. It raced towards the down ramp. The blonde woman who was driving seemed to be in complete control as she spun the wheel, and the car almost left the ground as they hurtled down the levels. "You okay?" she asked Summer.

"I'll tell you in a minute."

EIGHTEEN

IT'S SAID THAT we are born with two fears hard-wired into our minds by millions of years of evolution; the fear of loud noise and the fear of falling. Lock didn't buy it. Sure you could be startled by a sudden unexpected loud noise but he wasn't sure it qualified as a fear. People had a startle response, that was all. They weren't scared of loud noise in the way that they were of fears that they picked up along the way.

Falling was different. The dread of that lay in the anticipation, and anticipation was the key to fear. Even with a parachute and a reserve strapped to your back, falling was something that focused your mind, and right now, thought Lock, he was holding onto a man who desperately needed some focus in his life.

Dragging Jason by the collar of his jacket towards the edge of the building, Lock propelled him towards the concrete lip that faced the alleyway. He hustled him towards it the same way he would move a principal out of danger, quickly and with determination. Whatever Summer had done to him in the elevator had already sapped a lot of his energy. As they drew closer to the edge, Jason began to struggle. To settle him, Lock took his left thumb and jammed it as hard as he could into the thin cord of nerves at the hinge of Jason's jaw. Next he grabbed the actor's hand at the wrist and bent it back. Controlling someone in a situation like this was a matter of biomechanics and if Lock was to achieve what he needed without ending up facing a murder rap he would have to get this just right. With a hundred foot drop in play there was very little margin for error.

Lock shuffled Jason so that he was facing the building opposite. The actor's face grew pale as he contemplated the drop.

"I'll leave her alone, okay?" he said, his voice threatening to tip over into falsetto.

With his right hand still stressing Jason's wrist joint, Lock grabbed the actor's hair and yanked his head around so that he was looking at straight at him. "Too late, asshole. I have a very strict one-strike policy when it comes to guys like you and you've already had yours."

"The tape. Is that what this is about?"

Lock shook his head. "No, this is about you living in your little Hollywood bubble where everyone kisses your ass and you never have to face the consequences of your actions. Well, surprise, surprise, I don't care. You want to destroy someone I'm charged with protecting? Then I'm going to destroy you."

"You're not going to kill me," said Jason.

"You're right. I'm not. Gravity's going to take care of that," said Lock, using his right leg to sweep Jason's feet out from under him, and tilting him up and over the edge. Now there was more of the actor hanging over the edge than there was on the parking structure side of the concrete lip. His legs kicked out helplessly in mid air. The only thing that was preventing him plunging head first to the street below was Lock.

He began to sob. His face crumpled on itself, his bottom lip jutting outwards as tears welled in his eyes. Lock hoped that Ty was getting a good close up.

"Please, I'm begging you," said Jason. "I'll do anything you want me to. You name it. Just let me go."

"Anything?" Lock asked.

""Anything," sobbed the actor, fear completely overwhelming him as his body gave up all control and the smell of human faeces hit Lock's nostrils with a blast of warm air.

NINETEEN

Two Days Later

WITH TY DRIVING and Lock riding shotgun, the black Range Rover powered through Marina Del Rey. Summer sat in back with her manager. He handed her a sheaf of papers and a Mont Blanc fountain pen. She signed them with a flourish that signaled obvious relief.

"Okay, we're done," said Bernstein.

The papers were joint non disclosure agreements between her and Jason. Lock had brokered the detente. In return for Jason destroying the intimate footage of Summer, Lock did the same with the footage that he had showing the Hollywood tough guy breaking down to the point where he had soiled himself. The word blackmail had been bandied about at some length to no great effect. As far as Lock was concerned, Jason had started it and he had finished it. No one wanted to see this mess in court, no matter how much noise they made.

Of course none of that was mentioned in the legal documents. The wording was more general and related to an agreement between the two stars that they would not, under any circumstances, discuss their relationship or indeed release any material that related to their time together, either directly or via a third party. That also covered the pictures of Summer's injuries. As far as Lock was concerned, Jason had got a damn good deal.

Summer's manager, Bernstein, looked up from the paperwork. "I don't know how you got him to agree to this, Mr. Lock, but thank you."

Lock shrugged. "Sometimes all people need is a little perspective. It's a long way to the top but you can get back down pretty quick. I think Mr. Durham realized that."

Ty choked back a laugh, covering it by coughing into his hand. "Sorry, must be this air conditioning."

Next to Bernstein, Summer looked like a young woman with the weight of the world lifted from her shoulders. She was flying out to join the cast of her new movie. She could move on with her life. Apart from whoever did Jason's laundry, everyone was pretty much a winner.

"I hope you and your fiancee enjoy Malibu," Summer said to Lock.

"Thanks. We're looking forward to it," said Lock.

"You're an adorable couple," she added.

Lock smiled to himself. "I know. I'm a lucky man."

THE END

ABOUT THE AUTHOR

To research the Ryan Lock series of thrillers, Sean Black has trained as a bodyguard with former members of the Royal Military Police's specialist close protection unit, spent time inside America's most dangerous maximum security prison, Pelican Bay Supermax in California, and undergone desert survival training in Arizona.

A graduate of Columbia University in New York, he also holds a degree in Politics and Economics from Oxford University, England. The Ryan Lock books have been translated into Dutch, German and Russian, with a Spanish translation of the latest book in the series, The Devil's Bounty, scheduled for 2013, from the translator of The Kite Runner.

For more information on Sean Black and his books, see his website at www.seanblackbooks.com

THE RYAN LOCK SERIES
IN ORDER

Lockdown
Deadlock
Gridlock
The Devil's Bounty

3193042R00036

Printed in Great Britain
by Amazon.co.uk, Ltd.,
Marston Gate.